THE ADVENTURES
HERB
THE WILD TURKEY

HERB GOES CAMPING

To Andrew...
Enjoy Herb's Adventure!
Kristy Cameron
-2013"

This story is dedicated to my
husband, John, who to this day
is convinced there was a turkey
outside the cabin door.
-Kristy Cameron

Written by Kristy Cameron
Illustrated by Ian Shickle

ISBN-13   978-0-9859790-0-3

"Herb, please be careful! Turkey's can't climb trees," yelled Herb's mother from the other side of the campsite.

"Uh oh," yelped Herb, as he came crashing down to the ground.

He pulled his skinny body up out of the dirt and brushed off his dusty grey feathers.

Herb knew his mother had said not to wonder off, so he started exploring the campsite.

Herb started hopping over
pinecones toward the picnic table.

On the other side of the picnic
table, he noticed a narrow, dirt trail
leading out of their campsite
into some tall trees.

"I wonder what is at the end
of that trail?" thought Herb.

He was so curious about what was down the path, that he forgot what his mother had told him about staying in camp.

As he started following the trail, Herb's thin, knobby legs brushed against the prickly, green plants that hung over the path.

He gobbled happily as he strutted along.

The warm sun shined down on Herb making him grateful for his hat.

His red wattle swung back and forth as he looked from one side of the trail to the other.

"What a great day!" shouted Herb as he bounced along.

When he rounded the next bend, he looked up in awe because right in front of him was a BIG log cabin.

"Ooooh, I wonder what's in there?" he whispered to himself.

Herb crept across the yard and peeked up over the wooden deck.

The front door was open, and he saw a man, stretched out asleep, on a comfortable looking sofa.

Herb wanted to have some fun so he thought for a minute.

"I know," Herb thought to himself, " I'll see what happens if I wake him up."

Herb tiptoed up to the deck and peeked over the edge.

"Gobble, Gobble, Gobble," he quietly said.

Then he quickly ducked his head below the deck so the man wouldn't see him. The man stirred slightly.

Herb poked his head up and saw that
the man was still asleep.

"I'll have to try harder," he said quietly.
Herb tried again with more strength
in his voice.

"Gobble, Gobble, Gobble."

He tucked his head down just in time
and giggled to himself.

The man opened his eyes halfway,
looked at the door, saw nothing,
and went back to sleep.

"Hmmm," thought Herb "this is going to be harder than I thought."

Herb pulled himself up on to the deck, stood on his turkey tippy toes, took a *deeeeep* breath, and let out a huge,

"GOBBLE, GOBBLE, GOBBLE!"

It was loud enough to shake the whole cabin!

The man was so surprised; he jumped to his feet and screamed.

Herb was so surprised, he forgot to duck!

The man ran out the door and over to Herb. Herb stood frozen looking up at the man.

The man leaned forward and frowned. Herb gave the man a dashing turkey grin.

The man was so close that his hot breath moved Herb's red wattle back and forth.

(Now we know that Herb is a brave little turkey, but in this case...he yelled for his mother.)

"MOM!"

He jumped down off of the deck flapping his wings, fast and furious, trying to get away from the man.

Herb started running down the path. His knobby knees knocking against each other trying to go faster and faster.

Little sweat beads were spraying off of his face. He glanced back over his tail-feathers and saw the man running down the path after him. Herb's heart started beating wildly as he saw the man getting closer.

Herb poured on a burst of speed just as the man's hand closed around Herb's tail-feathers. "Ouch!" he gobbled.

One last look back showed the man standing in the path, holding all of Herb's handsome tail-feathers in his hand... looking rather pleased.

Herb kept running until he got back to the edge of his campsite.

"Yikes," he panted, "how am I going to explain this to Mom?"

He pulled his hat off and scratched his head wondering what to do.

"I'm going to be in so much trouble when Mom sees my missing tail-feathers."
He stood, on the path, staring at his hat.

"That's it!"

Herb took his hat, placed it on his bald bottom and then, grinning his most charming turkey grin, carefully walked into camp.

Herb saw his mom looking at him as he walked across their campsite.

"Herb," his mom said, "didn't I ask you to stay in camp?"

"Yes Mom," Herb answered as he scratched his turkey toe on the ground.

Herb's eyes grew big as he watched his mom look from his hatless bald head, to the hat hanging on his hiney.

"Mom, how fast do tail-feathers grow?" Herb asked, with a dazzling grin shining toward his mom. It didn't work. Herb's mom frowned.

"Not fast enough," she said,
"What happened to your tailfeathers?"

Herb told his mom how he lost his tail-feathers. As his mom listened, her face took on a surprised look.

"Mom, I wish I had listened to you and stayed in camp." said Herb with his wobbly chin pointing to the ground.

"I was really scared."

His mom pulled him in for a giant turkey hug. As she looked over his wing to the hat sitting on his bottom, she shook her head and a smile slowly began creeping onto her face.

Herb felt the safe warmth of his mother's wings wrapped around him. He Let out a big turkey sigh, happy to be back in his campground.

Herb began walking across the campsite, his hat swinging back and forth on his hiney as he walked.

Knowing what a close call he had today... Herb thought his tent sounded like the next perfect adventure.

About the Author... Kristy Cameron

Kristy was born in Portland, Oregon and loved writing at a young age. Although she has her Marketing and Advertising/Management degree, her first love is writing children's books. Kristy's book ideas stem from her fun loving family.

"I hope you will continue to laugh at Herb's antics when he makes a trip to the beach in an upcoming book!"

About the Illustrator... Ian Shickle

Ian grew up in Hedgesville, West Virginia, doodling night and day. Guess what? He never stopped...and now there are a few children's books as proof. In the end, the point of his work is nothing more than to make people smile.

You can follow our books at www.LPPublishing.net - Enjoy!

CPSIA information can be obtained
at www.ICGtesting.com
Printed in the USA
LVIC041231101112
306616LV00006B

* 9 7 8 0 9 8 5 9 7 9 0 0 3 *